The ADAM JOSHUA Capers

#1 The Monster in the Third Dresser Drawer

#2 The Kid Next Door

#3 Superkid!

#4 The Show-and-Tell War

#5 The Halloween Monster

#6 George Takes a Bow-Wow!

#7 Turkey Trouble

#8 The Christmas Ghost

And Coming Soon

...lson in Love

...rious Science

...e Baby Blues

The ADAM JOSHUA Capers

The Christmas Ghost

By Janice Lee Smith
Illustrated by Dick Gackenbach

HarperTrophy
A Division of HarperCollinsPublishers

ø cc 05

Previously published as There's a Ghost in the Coatroom:
Adam Joshua's Christmas

The Christmas Ghost
Text copyright © 1991 by Janice Lee Smith
Illustrations copyright © 1991 by Dick Gackenbach

Trophy ISBN 0-06-442022-1
First Harper Trophy edition, 1995.

To my father, James E. Lee—
always my favorite Christmas Spirit,
especially in a Santa suit.

BACK, back, back in Old England, when the King and Queen wanted to celebrate Christmas, they didn't fool around about it.

They sent out royal invitations, ordered the castle decked in its finest, and set their cooks to cooking like crazy.

All the knights in the kingdom polished up their armor and the stories of the brave things they'd done.

All the ladies got out their tall pointy hats and their party shoes.

And everybody came to a grand and glorious, truly spectacular feast.

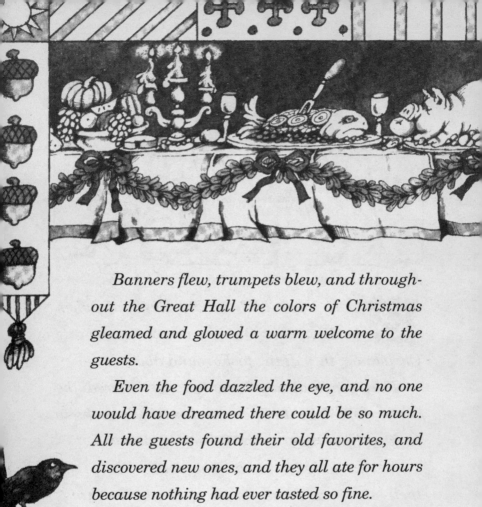

Banners flew, trumpets blew, and throughout the Great Hall the colors of Christmas gleamed and glowed a warm welcome to the guests.

Even the food dazzled the eye, and no one would have dreamed there could be so much. All the guests found their old favorites, and discovered new ones, and they all ate for hours because nothing had ever tasted so fine.

While everyone feasted, the King's jesters cracked them up with jokes, and magicians astonished them with magic tricks. Storytellers,

singers, and all sorts of other entertainers made sure that each and every guest had a wonderful time.

It was a night to remember always, a celebration full of laughter and love, a gift of joy and friendship.

And on the night before the night before Christmas, as a special gift for their parents, Adam Joshua's class was planning to have one just like it. . . .

Chapter One

. . . E xcept everyone wanted to be the King or Queen.

"So we'd better decide," laughed their teacher, Ms. D.

Everybody in the class sat still and tall and tried to look royal.

Angie patted her hair to get it ready for a crown.

Sidney ran a finger over his lip to smooth a mustache where a mustache would be if he had a mustache.

Adam Joshua tried to look wise and kingly.

"We'll have a vote," Ms. D. said. "Any nominations?"

There were a lot of nominations.

Adam Joshua nominated his best friend, Nelson, and in return Nelson nominated Adam Joshua.

Sidney nominated himself.

"I'm the best man for the job," he told them.

Ms. D. had them each write down the names of the King and Queen they chose.

Everyone, even the people who didn't get nominated, wrote down their own name and just let it go at that.

"Somehow, I don't think this is going to work," Ms. D. said, chuckling as she read the slips of paper. "So I'll tell you what," she said. "I have to run down and see when we can start getting extra time in the art

 6

room. When I get back, we'll just draw names for the King and Queen."

Everybody groaned, but Sidney put so much energy into it he fell off his chair.

———

While Ms. D. was gone, everybody sat around feeling grumpy, grouchy, gloomy, disappointed, and depressed. No one could remember their name ever being the name that got drawn for anything great.

In fact, as far as Adam Joshua could remember, his name usually just got drawn for things that were disgusting.

"You know," Angie finally said, "if I can't be the Queen, I don't want anybody else to be the Queen."

She glared at the rest of the girls, and they all glared back.

"So," she said, "why don't we have Ms. D. be Queen?"

Everybody thought about it for a minute.

"Actually," Heidi said, "it might be kind

of nice. Especially since she's going to have a baby and everything."

All the girls sighed and nodded.

"That's great!" said Philip. "And we can have Mr. D. be King. He's been doing a ton of stuff for us all year. I'd feel really good about it if he was the King."

Adam Joshua thought he would have felt a whole lot better about it if he'd been the King himself. But if it had to be somebody else, Mr. D. was probably best.

Everybody but Sidney muttered and moaned, griped and groaned, and voted to have Mr. and Ms. D. be the King and Queen.

"And I vote for Sidney," Sidney said, stretching his hand up high.

———

Ms. D. was very flattered.

"And delighted, and I thank you," she said. "I'm sure Mr. D. will feel the same, but you can surprise him yourself when he comes to pick me up after school."

"I'll bet kings get every single thing they ask for on their Christmas lists," Sidney grumbled, looking like his mustache would be drooping now if he had a mustache.

———

Once they'd found out they weren't going to be the King or Queen, and they'd quietly sulked about it long enough, everybody started getting excited about being a knight or a lady, or something else truly wonderful.

"And what's it to be?" Ms. D. asked, having them line up to tell her while she took notes.

Adam Joshua let a lot of other people go ahead of him so he could think. Ms. D. had told them to think about it yesterday, but he'd never gotten much past King.

"I'm going to be one of the ladies with a tall pointed hat," Heidi told Ms. D. when it was her turn. "But just the hat. I want to wear jeans."

"And I'll be a magician," Nelson said

happily. "I've learned a whole bunch of great new magic tricks with my fish. The parents are going to love them."

"I'm sorry, Nelson," Ms. D. said, "but I don't think we'd better have trick fish at the feast."

"Okay," Nelson told her sadly. "But it won't be the same, and the parents are going to feel really bad."

"Exotic Gypsy fortune-teller," Martha told Ms. D.

"Martha," Ms. D. said, "I'm not sure Old English feasts had exotic Gypsy fortune-tellers."

"This one's going to," Martha told her firmly. "And I'll even bring Reba, my snake, to help out."

"Okay on the fortune-telling," Ms. D. said. "Absolutely not on the snake."

"Once a person's a Queen, they sure get pushy," Martha grumbled, stomping away.

"We're the Three Musketeers," Jonesy

and Philip and Nate lined up to tell Ms. D.

"Boys," Ms. D. said. "I think Old England's probably the wrong time and place for the Musketeers. King Arthur had knights."

"Well, you can call us knights, and we'll dress like knights and do knight stuff all night," Nate told her. "But mostly we'll be the Three Musketeers."

"In disguise," said Jonesy.

"In case bad guys show up," said Philip.

"And the King needs us," said Nate.

"It's a deal," laughed Ms. D.

Adam Joshua had just decided to be a knight when Elliot Banks shoved his way into line ahead of him.

"I'll be the King's best knight," Elliot told Ms. D. smugly. "I can probably get a real suit of armor, and everybody else is just making their costume from stuff at home. My family has a real coat of arms, and all the other knights are just making

11

things up to put on their shields. I'll look the best"—Elliot smirked—"so it's only fair I should get to be the best knight. The King is going to be embarrassed to have any of those other guys by his side."

"I don't think the King plays favorites, Elliot," Ms. D. said.

"Well, he should," Elliot told her as he moved along. "I could probably even get a horse."

"What's it to be, Adam Joshua?" Ms. D. asked him next, sounding a tad weary. "And make it easy."

What was easy was knowing there was no way in the world he was going to be a knight with Elliot Banks around trying to be the best one. "Jester," Adam Joshua told her. Actually, he would have gone with jester first, but he thought the pictures of the costume looked a little skimpy, and he wasn't in the habit of showing his knees off to people. Still, he loved to tell jokes, and he didn't get an audience to sit still for them all that often.

"Terrific," Ms. D. said, writing it down. "You tell great jokes."

Adam Joshua was pleased she'd remembered. He wished she'd also remembered that he was best when he had his dog, George, telling jokes with him. Still, she'd just said "no" to fish, snakes, and horses, so it probably wasn't the time to ask.

Sidney was right behind him.

"Your Queenship," Sidney said with a bow, "I'm going to be the King-of-Some-Place-Else. Probably the King of this country would love a friend King to come visit him for Christmas."

"Good try," Ms. D. said. "But only one King per feast."

"Okay," Sidney told her, his no-mustaches bristling. "But the King's going to be really mad when he finds out you wouldn't let his best friend come over to eat."

14

Chapter Two

Just as school was ending for the day, Mr. D. came staggering in the door, buried under a stack of material and art supplies.

"Never try to work at home," his voice said from somewhere behind the stack, "with a pregnant pushy person around. You end up doing everything but your work."

Everybody crowded around to unstack him and tell him he was a king.

"Well, I'm deeply honored," he said. "And I thank you very much."

"You should," muttered Sidney.

"You'll have to wear a crown and cloak," Angie told him.

"Absolutely," said Mr. D.

"And you'll have to march into the Great Hall, and make a toast, and do king stuff all night."

"Naturally," Mr. D. said, sounding nicely kingly.

"Okay, then," Angie said, and most of them nodded, satisfied.

The Musketeers showed Mr. D. their Super-Deluxe King's-Secret-Spy Handshake.

"If you need spy stuff done, we're your men," said Jonesy.

"Day or night," said Philip. "Night or day."

"Except during school," said Nate.

"Also," Jonesy told Mr. D., "we need to

know your secret symbol. That way, when you need us, you send a messenger with your symbol, and we'll know it's really you."

"And not some evil king trying to trick us," Philip said.

"You guys must watch an awful lot of late-night TV," Mr. D. told them, sorting through his pockets and coming out with a gum wrapper. He tore it in two, and gave one half to the Musketeers, and put the other back in his pocket.

"Not gold," Jonesy said, disappointed.

"Close enough," said Nate.

———

Ms. D. sent Mr. D. out to bring in more stacks, and she shooed everyone else into the coatroom to get ready to go home.

There was something about the coatroom that brought out the Christmas list in all of them.

"I've sent my list to Santa Claus three

17

times," Ralph said. "And to my grand-parents twice."

Everybody in the room nodded. Adam Joshua had also sent his to Superman.

As the weather was getting colder, coats were getting fatter, and the coatroom was getting a lot harder to get many people into.

Everyone started to push.

"I even sent my list to the President," Philip said, trying to reach around Angie for his coat.

Everybody stopped shoving for a minute to think about whether they knew the President's address.

As soon as the ruckus started again, Philip tripped and fell into Angie, and Angie got ready to bop him.

"No fighting, no biting," a deep, low voice said.

Angie stopped in mid bop, and looked around and looked scared.

"Also no thrashing, bashing, mashing, or hitting with book bags," said the voice.

Philip, and everybody who'd been watching the bopping with interest, started looking scared too.

"I think it's a ghost," Doug whispered.

"But it's not Halloween or anything," whispered Nelson.

"Maybe it's the ghost of the Christmas Spirit," Angie said, worried. "I saw a play about that once with this awfully mean man named Scrooge in it. He was really grouchy and grumpy about Christmas, and greedy and everything, so a lot of ghosts haunted him."

"We've been a little grumpy and greedy," Heidi whispered.

"And grouchy," whispered Angie.

Adam Joshua had a terrible sinking feeling in the pit of his stomach. It seemed to him, on second thought, that maybe it had been a little greedy to ask for a motorcycle on his Christmas list.

"Excuse me," Angie called out, trying to sound polite and brave at the same time, "are you the Christmas Spirit ghost?"

"Sounds good to me," said the ghost.

"We didn't mean to be grumpy or greedy," Angie said, nervously looking over her shoulder and behind her back.

"Hmmm," said the ghost.

Adam Joshua was starting to think that asking for the giant-screen TV had been a mistake too.

"Besides," Heidi said, "we're making up for it by giving our parents a Christmas feast, and we're going to work at it really hard so they'll have a great time, and we'll try to have a lot of Christmas spirit."

"That'll make up for it, won't it?" Angie asked, eyeing the row of coats nervously.

"We'll have to see," said the ghost.

———

Everybody fell over everybody else trying to get out of the coatroom, and the minute Mr. D. staggered back in the door, they tackled him, stacks and all.

It took a bit to get him sorted out and on his feet again, but as soon as they told him about the coatroom, he drew himself up to his full height and looked tough.

"I," he told them, "am a master ghost hunter, ghost chaser, and ghost bopper. You got a ghost? I'm the guy to call."

Everybody grabbed Mr. D., pushed him into the coatroom, and pulled the door shut after him.

Then they all gathered around and tried to listen through the door.

"Shouldn't you guys be in there with him?" Heidi asked the Musketeers.

"It's one for all," said Jonesy.

"And all for one," said Philip.

"But nobody if it's ghosts," said Nate.

They could hear Mr. D. singing

 22

"Rudolph's My Red-Nosed Ghost, Dear."

They could hear him singing "Jingle Ghost Rock." He'd just started "Silver Ghosts" when he yelled "Yikes!" and got quiet.

"It got him," Angie said sadly.

"I'll have to be King," Sidney said, sadly too.

Adam Joshua felt really awful. He couldn't believe that just because he'd asked for a swimming pool, they'd lost Mr. D.

When the door suddenly flew open, half of them fell into the coatroom, and the other half, including the Musketeers, ran screaming away.

"No problem," Mr. D. said, dusting off his hands. "No more ghost."

"What did it look like?" Heidi asked nervously.

"Big," Mr. D. told her. "Ugly. Green."

"The Christmas Spirit was green?"

Angie asked, sounding surprised.

"That was the Christmas Spirit?" Mr. D. looked amazed. "Gosh. Really? How do you know?"

"Because we were grouchy," Heidi told him.

"Disgusting," sighed Mr. D.

"And grumpy," Doug told him.

"Outrageous," said Mr. D.

"And greedy," said Adam Joshua.

"Unbelievable," said Mr. D.

He thought about it a minute.

"Greedy, how?" he asked.

"We put too many things on our Christmas lists," Angie told him. "And sent our lists to Santa too many times."

"Well, hey," Mr. D. said, dropping his voice to a whisper so Ms. D. wouldn't overhear. "I personally sent my own list to the President."

Everybody lined up to pound him on the back and shake his hand.

Chapter Three

When Adam Joshua and Nelson walked to school the next morning, the sweet certain smell of snow was in the air.

"I don't think I can handle the first big snow, a ghost in the coatroom, and learning new magic tricks without my fish all at the same time," Nelson said glumly.

Adam Joshua nodded. If you kept the snow and the ghost, made it new jokes without a dog, and added in Christmas-list-greed guilt, he felt exactly the same way.

Angie and Sidney caught up with them as they walked.

"The weather woman says to get ready for inches of snow," Angie said anxiously, and they all shivered with the thought of something that had nothing at all to do with ghosts or the cold.

They were a little early, so there weren't many people in the classroom yet, and there were even fewer in the coatroom.

Angie tiptoed in through the coatroom door, Adam Joshua and Nelson crept, and Sidney did a sort of sneaky-slide Sidney step.

Adam Joshua hung his coat as quickly as he could and started to back back out the door.

"How's it going?" asked the voice.

Somebody's teeth started chattering, and Adam Joshua had a feeling it wasn't the ghost's.

"Is that it again?" Sidney asked in a shaky voice. "I thought Mr. D. said he ghost-blasted it."

"Didn't take," chuckled the ghost.

Adam Joshua groaned. He'd sent out a letter last night canceling most of his Christmas list, and he'd marked it "Special Delivery," but the mailman probably hadn't known which coatroom he'd meant.

"You know," Angie whispered, "it could be Santa Claus. You know that part about 'sees you when you're sleeping, knows when you've been bad or good'?"

"It could be Santa Claus's ghost," said Nelson.

"Oh my gosh, oh my gosh!" Sidney yelped. "Santa Claus died and nobody told us. It stands to figure he'd die. He's been around for ages, and he's really old.

"Oh my gosh, oh my gosh!" Sidney moaned, running around the coatroom in circles and smacking himself on the fore-head with his hand. "If Santa Claus is dead, who's going to get my list? Who's going to bring me all that stuff? I didn't figure I'd get most of it anyway, but if Santa's dead, I don't stand a chance of getting much of it at all."

Sidney fell over his own foot and landed flat on the floor.

"Get up, Sidney," the ghost said. "And calm down."

Sidney got up very quietly and looked scared. Adam Joshua, Angie, and Nelson looked scared for him.

It was one thing to hear a ghost. It was another to hear a ghost call your name.

———

"Sorry," Mr. D. said when he got to school and they'd tackled and told him. He looked puzzled.

"I usually guarantee my work," he said. "But I guess it's better not to fool around

 28

with the Christmas Spirit."

"It may be Santa Claus's ghost instead," Sidney croaked in a rusty not-too-much-like Sidney voice.

"Well, then that does it," said Mr. D. "We definitely don't want to make this ghost mad. We'd better just learn to live with it."

He waved good-bye and left for home again.

"Easy for him to say," croaked Sidney.

———

Ms. D. settled everybody down and set them to work in the art room.

The ladies started making tall pointy hats, and the knights studied pictures of shields.

"I guess every family can't have a real coat of arms," Elliot said smugly. He made a big deal out of propping a copy of his up so that everybody had to walk past it any-time they wanted to walk anywhere in the

room, and a lot of the knights looked gloomy every time they did.

Adam Joshua started stringing bells on ribbon for his jester's costume and worrying about his knees.

Nelson cut moons and stars out of sparkly paper to glue on his magician's hat. After while he started cutting out some fish too.

Angie decided on a hamster for her coat of arms. She cut it out of felt, glued on jewels for eyes, and added more jewels for a collar.

"It's Walton Eight," Angie said, showing her shield to Adam Joshua and Nelson. "The only thing is"—Angie sighed—"he died last week, just like all my hamsters keep dying, and I don't know whether to make him alive or dead on my shield."

Adam Joshua and Nelson just nodded and looked sympathetic. It really didn't seem like a question you could answer for somebody else.

"I think dead's best," Angie said. "It's more truthful, and I'd hate for the coat-room ghost to think I think alive's better."

She glued the hamster on upside down, with its feet sticking up in the air. She drew a lot of flowers around it, added some more jewels and wrote Rest in Peace, Walton 8 on top.

"You know, actually he's much more interesting dead," Angie said, holding up her shield, pleased.

———

A little kid came into the art room late in the afternoon and held up half a gum wrapper.

"A guy outside said you'd know what this meant," he said, sounding puzzled.

The Three Musketeers fell over themselves and everybody else getting out the door. They came back groaning and carrying an enormous throne between them.

"I had a little spare time," Mr. D. said

modestly, bowing to the applause while the Musketeers lay on the floor panting.

"Also," Mr. D. told them, looking very regal, "I have decided to have a special King's mascot."

Everyone clustered close, and with a grand flourish, Mr. D. set a stuffed animal down on the art-room table and tried to fluff it up.

"My Most Royal Stuffed Moose, Morose," Mr. D. said proudly.

Morose looked limp and lumpy and like his fluffing days were long past.

"But he's adorable anyway," Angie told Mr. D., and everybody cheered.

The King was looking royally pleased with himself as he headed for the door.

"Forget something?" Ms. D. called after him.

It took Mr. D. a long time to think of it, but when he did he looked a little embarrassed.

"Oh, right," he said, hurrying off to build a throne for the Queen too.

———

"I've decided," Sidney told Adam Joshua, as everybody tromped back to the class-room and tried to get up their nerve to go into the coatroom, "it's Santa, not Santa's ghost or anything. So I'm going to read him my list to make sure he gets it all, and that way he can ask questions about the size of horse I want, and the color and everything.

"This will work great!" Sidney said, pulling out his long, rolled-up list.

"Santa and I want to be alone," he said happily, closing the coatroom door behind him.

Everybody waited nervously outside in the classroom.

"Maybe he shouldn't be in there by himself," Angie said.

"I don't think it's a dangerous ghost,"

Heidi told them. "I mean, I don't think it would make Sidney a ghost too or anything."

Everyone got quiet thinking about a coatroom always haunted by a Sidney ghost.

Sidney came out of the coatroom again, looking a little pale.

"I don't know who that is," he said, disgusted. "But it sure isn't Santa."

Chapter Four

Christmas came scurrying closer.

Everybody watched the sky nervously, but the snow held off.

Ms. D. shooed them away from the window for the umpteenth time.

"Morgan's Hill or no Morgan's Hill," she scolded them, "there's work to be finished if we're going to have this feast."

"Between the ghost and Morgan's Hill," Angie told her, worried, "we may never make it to the feast."

Even so, Ms. D. kept them working like crazy, and along with everything else they had to start practicing so they'd be ready to entertain.

Adam Joshua practiced his favorite jokes.

It wasn't easy without a dog.

Nelson practiced his magic tricks.

"They just aren't going well without the fish," he said sadly.

Sidney practiced being the Stand-in Back-up King.

"You may all bow," he kept telling everybody. "And call me 'Your Most-Super-Better-Than-Anybody-Else-Could-Possibly-Ever-Be-and-We're-Glad-to-Have-You Grand Majesty.'"

———

Since nobody knew how to get rid of it, it seemed like they were going to be stuck with a spirit in the coatroom.

And as long as they were stuck with it, Adam Joshua felt that maybe he'd better get busy and apologize, person to ghost.

He left the art room a little early one afternoon and hurried down the hall. The closer he got to the coatroom, the slower his hurry got, but he went in anyway and shut the door.

"You rang?" asked the ghost.

"I came to say I'm sorry," Adam Joshua said, trying to keep his voice from shaking and his knees from knocking and the entire rest of his body from falling apart.

"I mean I know I put too many things on my Christmas list," Adam Joshua said, trembling on. "And the race car seemed like a good idea at the time, but it probably wasn't such a good idea."

"Probably not," chuckled the ghost.

"Anyway," Adam Joshua whispered, "I'll try not to be that greedy ever again."

The ghost didn't say anything for a moment. Adam Joshua didn't know if it

was thinking or pulling itself together to do something awful.

There came a rapping at the coatroom door, and Adam Joshua screamed.

"Excuse me," Angie said, sticking her head into the coatroom. "I came to apologize for my Christmas list."

———

The ghost must have decided to forgive them.

"In fact, I think maybe he's starting to like us," Angie told Adam Joshua when she was finished with her turn in the coatroom. She looked really relieved, and she was chuckling a little. "He just told me the greatest joke."

A lot of people were getting back from the art room, and they nearly stampeded over Angie in order to hear the joke too.

"Thank goodness," Heidi said on her way past. "I was trying to get up my nerve to come apologize for my Christmas list."

Adam Joshua had never worked so hard getting ready for someone else to have a great Christmas, and he had a sneaking hunch that was exactly what Ms. D. had in mind when she thought up this feast in the first place.

Angie and Martha had to pull Sidney out of Mr. D.'s throne every time they needed to decorate it, and he was busy making a crown before anybody caught him at it.

"Cut that out!" Angie told him.

"I'm going to be the Just-in-Case-of-Emergencies King," Sidney told her. "Mr. D. might miss the feast. He might get caught in traffic, or he might have to go out of town on business, or he might walk out of his house, trip into the snow on a patch of ice somebody forgot, start rolling into a bigger and bigger snowball, and end up rolling into the ocean."

"Good grief!" Angie said, stomping away.

"He won't drown or anything," Sidney called after her. "But it'll take him an awfully long time to get back and dry off."

———

They were busy, but never too busy for the ghost.

After a while they figured out that he wasn't always in the coatroom.

Sometimes he was there right before school started in the mornings, and sometimes he was there when they were getting ready to go home in the afternoon, but other times they couldn't find him at all.

"There are probably an awfully lot of grumpy, grouchy, greedy people around," Angie said. "So the ghost is probably really busy."

Everybody shook their heads over the idea of there being so many grumpy, greedy people in the world.

"It's a good thing the Christmas Spirit has us to come home to," said Heidi.

"Otherwise he'd never get any rest."

He got to be so popular, Angie finally put a sheet of paper up on the coatroom door, and everyone had to sign up for a turn. But nobody paid any attention to it, and they all still crowded into the coatroom anytime the Christmas Spirit was there.

He told them a great joke about a ghost and a peanut-butter sandwich.

He told them a great joke about two spirits and a telephone pole.

"And why did the ghost cross the road?" he asked them.

He told them a fantastic joke about one of Santa's reindeer.

"I'm not naming names," the Christmas Spirit said, while they all howled. "But I promise that's a true story. I've got inside information."

"Knock, knock," said the ghost.

"Whooooooo's there?" everybody asked.

———

Suddenly and finally, after all the thinking it would never come and that they would never be ready if it did, it was the day before the day of the night before the night before Christmas.

"I still can't believe we're going to make it," Angie said, adding the final moose design to the throne.

And it started snowing. Fat fluffy flakes came floating steadily out of the sky and piled inches deep on the ground.

In the art room, they kept watch. The more snow fell, the quieter they got, and the louder the quiet sounded.

Finally they all walked over and looked solemnly out the window.

"There's enough," Nelson said, and they all looked at each other bravely and nodded.

———

"Okay," Ms. D. said at the end of the day. "Be here early tomorrow to get the cafeteria ready."

"Excuse me," Angie said, raising her hand. "But there's something we have to do first."

"Agreed," Ms. D. said, laughing. "You've worked so hard, we can take time out for a little modern tradition. You can come after Morgan's Hill."

Everyone bundled up in the coatroom getting ready to head home.

"I always get scared to pieces when I even think about going down Morgan's Hill for the first time," Angie said.

"I almost get sick to my stomach," said Heidi.

"I have nightmares about it all night the night before," Doug said, sighing.

"Then why do we keep doing it every year?" somebody asked, worried.

"I wouldn't miss it for the world," said Angie and Heidi and Doug.

"Whoooooooo's Morgan?" asked the ghost.

47

Chapter Five

The next morning, everybody stood at the top of Morgan's Hill looking down.

Nobody volunteered to go first.

Everybody but Sidney voted on Sidney.

"Why me?" he yelled, as they loaded him on the sled and got the sled in position.

Everybody but Sidney stayed quiet, watching.

Sidney hollered, and screamed, and fell off his sled halfway down, and finished in a spectacular roll to the bottom. He lay there panting for a minute.

"You just can't beat Morgan's Hill," he yelled up.

———

Everybody hollered and screamed, and fell off their sleds, and rolled into piles piled with everybody else.

"I love this hill," Heidi said from somewhere underneath Martha and Angie.

Adam Joshua went down feet first, and then he went down back first, and he would have gone down headfirst, but he was afraid he'd lose his head.

"Every year this is the bravest thing I do," Angie told him as they rested at the bottom of the hill. "And every year I think I'll never be this brave again, but I'm glad this year I was."

Doug came down trying to ride his sled like a skateboard.

Jonesy came down, trying to use Sidney for his sled.

"Oh, rats!" Heidi said. "Look."

Elliot Banks stood at the top of the hill, smirking down. Even though it wasn't even Christmas yet, he had a brand-new, super-shiny, bright-red bike sled. He had a matching helmet.

Everybody at the top of the hill moved back to give him room. Everybody at the bottom of the hill cleared out so they wouldn't get run over.

Elliot revved up even though he didn't have a motor. He straightened his helmet, and pulled down his goggles, and yelled, "Geronimo!"

He fell off halfway down the hill, and his sled went on without him.

"I just love Morgan's Hill," Heidi said, chuckling.

———

Mr. and Ms. D. showed up with a toboggan.

"Good grief!" Mr. D. said, tiptoeing over to the edge of the hill to peek down.

Ms. D. made him get on the toboggan, and everybody else stopped sledding and hurried over to give him a great push-off.

Sidney pushed extra.

Everybody but Mr. D. stayed at the top of the hill and watched quietly.

Mr. D. yelped, and yelled, and hollered, and screamed, and pleaded for mercy, and howled, "I want my moose!" He fell off his sled halfway down and finished the other half in a noisy but impressive roll.

He lay at the bottom of the hill moaning for a minute.

"Rats," Sidney said, looking down disgusted from the top. "He made it."

"Who the heck," Mr. D. finally yelled up, "was Morgan?"

———

Once Mr. D. got the hang of sledding down Morgan's Hill, it was hard to get him to stop.

"And he's really dangerous on that

thing," Angie said, diving out of the way of a zipping toboggan.

"Cowabunga, Morose!" Mr. D. kept yelling all the way down, and finally everybody had to help Ms. D. drag him off the hill.

"But I still want to meet that Morgan sometime," Mr. D. said firmly after they took his toboggan away.

———

When they got to school, the cafeteria looked like a cafeteria.

"And I don't think it's ever going to look like anything else," Angie told Ms. D., and they all nodded, discouraged.

"Have a little Christmas spirit," Ms. D. told them, laughing.

"I just checked—he's not here right now," said Heidi.

They got busy and decked the halls, the walls, the tables, and everything else that looked like it could use a good decking.

Too many people tried to help hold the ladder for Mr. D., and they left him hanging high with the banners.

"As King, I appoint Queen D. the Chief Ladder Holder," Mr. D. said, still shaking after they got him down.

Sidney didn't say anything, but he stood looking thoughtfully up at the banners for a long, long time.

———

After he'd recovered from the banners, Mr. D. hung up a kissing ball, with plenty of mistletoe in it.

"I'm not sure they had those in Old England," Sidney told him. "It's probably too new-fashioned."

Mr. D. grabbed Ms. D. on her way past, gave her a big dip backward, and kissed her before she knew what hit her.

Everybody closed their eyes.

"My goodness," Ms. D. said, looking surprised, then looking embarrassed, and

then smiling a little. By the time she walked away, she was looking pretty pleased.

"Old-fashioned," Mr. D. told Sidney, satisfied. "And in perfect working order."

———

"The Christmas Spirit is here now," Heidi called out just as Adam Joshua was trying to undeck himself from some decking that had gotten out of hand.

Everybody else stampeded down to the coatroom to hear the new jokes.

Adam Joshua finally got loose, and was hurrying down the hall to join them when he noticed something that he'd never paid a lot of attention to before. And it made him start thinking about something he'd never done a lot of thinking about before.

And all things considered, he thought he'd better get busy and investigate. By the time he came back, he was chuckling a little and worrying a lot about whether it was too

late to send his original Christmas list out
again.

———

"It looks absolutely wonderful," Ms. D.
told them at the end of the afternoon, as
they all stood—tired, happy, and proud—
looking at their Great Hall.

It really did.

Banners, most of them with drawings of
Morose, flew high. The reds and greens
and golds of Christmas gleamed and
glowed and shimmered from every corner.

All the tables looked like they were just
waiting for a feast to come by.

"Now for the final and most important
thing," Mr. D. said solemnly.

The Three Musketeers tried to hide, but
Mr. D. found them and made them follow
him to the art room. They came panting
back, carrying the King's throne between
them, and they placed it at the front of the
Great Hall.

Mr. D. had them move it three times, until it was sitting in the absolutely best spot, and he sat in it a few times himself to get the fit right, and he took Sidney out of it twice.

"Perfect," Mr. D. said, setting the Royal Moose, Morose, in the place of honor beside it.

"Forget something?" Ms. D. asked him as everybody started packing up to go home and get dressed.

"Nag, nag, nag," Mr. D. grumbled, sending the Musketeers down to bring Queen D.'s throne too.

Chapter Six

The school doors would have told you they'd seen just about everything there was to see come through them. But they'd never seen anything like the members of the King's Court who came walking in that evening.

Ladies moved gracefully in long floaty dresses and tall pointy hats. Heidi wore her hat with jeans and her cowboy boots.

Knights clunked and clanked a bit. Knight outfits weren't as easy to come by as floaty dresses, so people pretty well had to make do with what they could.

Tyler had wrapped himself in a lot of aluminum foil, and added a football helmet.

Ralph wore his Superman cape, set a cooking pot on his head, and had a stuffed dragon dragging behind him.

Elliot Banks had a fantastic silver toy helmet and a great toy sword.

"Wouldn't you know?" Tyler growled.

And Elliot's shield read MY REAL COAT OF ARMS across the top of his real coat of arms and his cape read THE KING'S BEST KNIGHT! across the back.

Nelson's magician's hat rose high, and the moon, stars, and fish sparkled mysteriously every time they caught the light.

Everybody kept whistling at Adam Joshua's knees.

King D. looked handsome and royal.

"Wow!" the girls said, giggling.

61

Queen D. looked beautiful and regal.

"Double wow!!" the boys whispered, totally awestruck.

It took a little while to get the parents to settle down, mostly because a lot of the fathers kept trying to catch a lot of the mothers under the kissing ball.

"Especially yours," Angie told Adam Joshua, sending him over to put a stop to it.

Finally they got all the parents calm and seated at their tables. They turned off the big lights, and turned on the little ones, and suddenly it didn't look like a school cafeteria anymore. It looked like the mysterious Great Hall of an ancient king.

Everyone floated, clanked, and sparkled over to start lining up for the King's Grand March.

The Queen made the Three Musketeers put away their wooden swords, after they'd nearly taken off several people's ears.

"But we may need them," Jonesy told her. "It's just like underwear. The Three Musketeers always wear their swords too."

"Bad guys always crash Christmas feasts," said Philip.

"When did we make that rule about underwear?" asked Nate.

All the guests in the Great Hall got politely quiet and watched the door.

Doug stepped up to one side of the doorway and blew his trumpet.

"The Grand March," he announced.

Ellen stepped up to the other side of the door and beat her drum.

The Royal Court was supposed to march around the room two times, but the leading knights and ladies liked the applause so much they led everyone around three.

"I could do this all evening," Heidi said, blowing kisses.

"I think we already have," Ralph grumbled, tripping over his dragon leash again.

Adam Joshua did his best to keep a jester's smile on his face, but it wasn't exactly easy with all the knee jokes going on.

———

Since nobody had chosen to be just a servant, everybody had to scurry once they got back outside the Great Hall to pitch in and help serve the food.

"Peanut-butter sandwiches!" Angie yelped when she saw Philip's tray. "You brought peanut-butter sandwiches?"

"Look," Philip growled. "We were supposed to bring food and I brought food. I know what they used to have, but I didn't know where to catch an ox, and I didn't want to cook a hog, and Ms. D. said to bring something we knew how to fix without much help, and I knew how to make peanut-butter sandwiches."

"I made them too," Sidney told Angie

proudly. "Only I used a cookie cutter, and all my sandwiches look like pigs."

Doug blew his trumpet. Ellen beat her drum.

"The traditional foods," Doug boomed, "were roast ox, stuffed boar, all sorts of fish and fowl, soups, fruits, cakes, puddings . . ." Sidney went past him with the first tray.

"And peanut-butter sandwiches," Doug said, without missing a beat. "Some shaped like pigs."

After the sandwiches came trays of popcorn, candy canes, apple cider, and cookies.

Adam Joshua took his dad a lot of everything to keep his mind off the kissing ball.

"This is definitely my kind of party," Sidney's father said, taking triple doubles on the pigs.

Before the feasting began, King D. stood regally and raised his cup for a toast.

Everyone else stood, and all raised their cups with him.

"Good people, lovely ladies, brave knights and my Queen," said the King. "To the joy and friendship of Christmas."

"To joy and friendship," everyone said, drinking deeply.

Everybody sat back down.

Sir Sidney stood and raised his cup.

"Good kids, and everybody else," he said.

The kids all stood and raised their cups, and most of the parents stood too, but they looked confused.

"To Morgan's Hill," said Sidney. "And the Christmas Spirit."

A rousing cheer went up and around and through the Great Hall, until it shook the rafters and reached down the hall to the coatroom, and the kids drained their cups of apple cider dry.

Chapter Seven

As soon as they'd served the feast foods, the servers hurried back outside the Hall and turned themselves into entertainers.

"The King and Queen sure have it easy," Angie said, looking around for her shield with its hamster coat of arms. "They just get to sit there on their thrones, eat, and look great all night."

"Grr," said Sir Sidney.

Adam Joshua helped Tyler put more

tape on his aluminum foil to keep it in place.

Elliot Banks polished his helmet and polished his sword, held his shield high, fluffed out his cape, and did his best to look like the King's best knight.

Martha reached into her basket and took out her crystal ball, and her snake, Reba.

Several brave knights let out screams and headed the other direction in a hurry.

Martha wrapped Reba around her shoulders, tucked her crystal ball under her arm, adjusted her turban, and marched into the Great Hall to tell fortunes.

"I think we'd better wait a minute," Angie said.

Everybody waited patiently.

It wasn't long before the sound of a lot of commotion came from the Great Hall, and a minute later the doors burst open, and a lot of parents came rushing out.

"Martha loses that snake every time," Angie said, sighing.

There was a terrible bloodcurdling, screeching, reaching scream from inside the Hall.

"King D.," Angie said, sighing some more.

Everybody looked at the Musketeers.

"We don't do snakes," Philip said, and the other Musketeers shook their heads firmly.

It sounded like a great pandemonium in the Great Hall, and then Martha came out the door again, with a disgusted-looking Reba slung over her arm and a fierce-looking Queen right behind.

Martha got Reba tucked back in her basket. "Poor baby," she said, kissing Reba on the nose. "Did that bad King scare you?"

The Queen got the guests back to their tables. She made King D. climb down from where he was standing on the seat of his throne.

71

"Why is it," he said shakily, not sounding the least bit kingly, "that whenever that snake's around, it always heads straight for me?"

"Love," the Queen told him.

"Now we can go in," Angie said, cheerfully leading the way.

"Rats," Sidney sighed, taking his Just-in-Case-of-Emergencies crown off the top of his head again.

———

"I had to bring three of my fish too," Nelson whispered to Adam Joshua as they followed everyone into the Great Hall. "But don't worry. None of them will get loose and go after the King. My fish Marilyn says he just isn't her type at all."

Everybody spread out to entertain the guests while they feasted.

The knights and ladies of the court formed into small groups and walked around singing softly.

"Silver Bells," Angie and Heidi and Ellen sang.

"Silver Ghosts," sang the Three Musketeers.

"Great Green Globs of Greasy, Grimy Gopher Guts," sang Sidney, and several parents turned green themselves and stopped eating.

———

Martha gave a great sigh, tried to look tragic and snakeless, tucked her crystal ball under her arm, straightened her turban, and marched off once again to tell fortunes.

She made the first stop at her own parents.

"This is amazing," she said, looking in her crystal ball.

"You're going to give your daughter everything she's asked for on her Christmas list."

"Really?" said Martha's father. "Who would have thought?"

"Especially the horse," Madam Majesta Martha told him.

"First the snake goes," her father said firmly, "then we talk."

Nelson was keeping well out of Queen D.'s sight with his magic fish tricks.

"But everybody else loves them," Nelson told Adam Joshua happily when their paths crossed.

Adam Joshua sighed. Everybody would have loved George too.

He went to tell jokes in front of the King.

"Why did a ghost cross the road?" Adam Joshua asked.

"Surely you jest," laughed King D.

The Three Musketeers came, dragging Sidney tied up behind them.

They presented him to the King.

"Your Majesty," Jonesy said, bowing, "we caught a bad guy."

Adam Joshua helped out by sitting on Sidney.

"Mmm," King D. said, looking serious. "What was he up to?"

"Cutting out sandwiches shaped like pigs," said Jonesy.

"Putting too many things on his Christmas list," said Philip.

"Making us listen a thousand times to his Christmas list," said Nate.

The King thought for a little while.

Sidney started looking scared and started getting a lot wigglier, and Adam Joshua had to sit a lot harder.

"Since it's Christmas," King D. said, "and we're in a party mood, we're going to let him off."

"Darn!" said Jonesy and Philip and Nate.

Adam Joshua untied Sidney and fluffed him up again.

"Would you like to hear my Christmas

list?" Sidney asked the King, pulling up a chair to sit beside him.

———

Adam Joshua found some markers and had Angie draw laughing faces on his knees.

Then he went and jested for his parents and a lot of other parents, and for the Three Musketeers, who were all looking pretty depressed that no bad guys besides Sidney had shown up.

He jested his way over to be near Nelson.

Nelson started doing magic tricks for Elliot Banks's father. Elliot swaggered over, pushed his way in on the bench beside his father, and banged his cider mug down on the table to let Nelson know that the King's best knight had arrived.

Nelson did a great trick with just his one fish, Elvis.

"Very nice," said Elliot's father.

"Stupid," snickered Elliot.

Nelson did a hard trick with both Elvis and Marilyn.

"Impressive," said Elliot's father.

"Boring," sneered Elliot.

Nelson did a very complicated, almost impossible, trick using Elvis, Marilyn, and Houdini all at once.

"Amazing," said Elliot's father.

"Dumb, dumb, dumb," yawned Elliot.

Elliot's father turned his head for a second to catch something a father beside him was saying. Elliot shoved his head between theirs to listen in.

Nelson lost control of his fish, and Houdini went jumping high and landed in Elliot's mug.

And before Houdini could yell for help, Elliot picked up the mug and drank it dry.

Nelson and Adam Joshua stood looking at Elliot in horror. They didn't say a thing because there didn't seem to be much to say.

78

Elvis and Marilyn didn't say anything either.

"Only two fish left!" Elliot's father exclaimed, turning his attention back to the magic tricks. "You made one disappear. Very, very good!"

Houdini no doubt knew he'd been swallowed by Elliot, but Elliot didn't seem to have a clue he'd swallowed Houdini.

"Stupid, stupid, very stupid," he just said, smirking and swaggering away again.

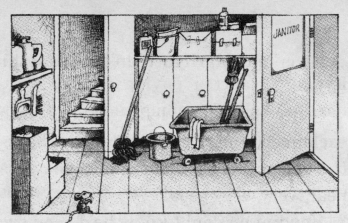

Chapter Eight

King and Queen D. started to move around among the feasters so they could talk to everyone.

"I'm a king of the people," King D. told them.

As soon as the King was out of his throne, Sidney whipped out his crown and moved in.

"Capture the Three Musketeers," he ordered several knights. "And throw them in the dungeon."

 80

Everyone started paying Martha to tell fortunes for their moms and dads.

She made Sidney pay extra.

"You will make sure Sidney gets a helicopter for Christmas," she told his parents while she studied her crystal ball.

"You must have the wrong channel on that thing," Sidney's father said.

"There's more," Martha said, unrolling Sidney's list.

"There would be," his father said, sighing.

———

Nelson had moaned something that sounded like "Arrguhh, Houdini!" and disappeared for a while himself.

Adam Joshua finally found him sitting in a corner, looking miserable.

"I am never, ever, never going to use my fish in magic tricks again, Adam Joshua," Nelson said. "It's just too dangerous for them."

Adam Joshua tried to think of a joke about disappearing fish to cheer Nelson up.

"I thought Elliot might die or something," Nelson said. "So I told Queen D. She said he won't die. She said she'd tell his parents. She said we're going to have a long talk soon about responsibility.

"I told her there was no hurry." He got up to get back to work. "My fish Elvis is very depressed," Nelson sighed. "He said he's always heard about people eating raw fish, but he never thought he'd see it happen to one of his friends."

———

By the time King D. got back to his throne, King Sidney was well settled in.

"No, no, don't get up," King D. told him, pulling up a chair.

"I wasn't planning on it," King Sidney told him.

"It's only fair you should get to be King for a while," King D. said, putting Morose in Sidney's lap. "Especially with all the Royal Chores to do."

King Sidney might have been short, but he wasn't dumb.

"What Royal Chores?" he asked suspiciously.

"Saying good night to the guests, putting out the moose, undecking all the decking we decked earlier," King D. said, thoughtfully counting things off on his fingers.

King Sidney nodded, relieved.

"Helping with the dishes," King D. went on, "eating the leftover candy canes, kissing the Queen."

King Sidney was out of the throne in a flash.

"Does it every time," King D. told Morose.

———

The evening started wrapping up just about the time Tyler's aluminum-foil armor started unwrapping.

83

The Three Musketeers gathered around and sang him a song from a TV commercial about using plastic wrap the next time instead.

"That thing was a terrible idea," Angie told Adam Joshua as they tried to get the parents back past the kissing ball and out the door.

They all stopped in their tracks when they heard a blood-chilling, bone-chilling, back-of-the-neck-chilling screech.

The Three Musketeers happily headed in three different directions to rescue the King.

"Don't worry," Angie told everybody else. "It's just Elliot. I saw Queen D. tell his parents something, and then they called him over and told him something, and now he just keeps yelling something about a fish and shouting, 'Someday, somehow, someplace I'll get you for this, Nelson!'"

Nelson did a great vanishing act into an empty classroom, and he stayed there until Elliot's parents had taken a screeching Elliot out of the cafeteria and out of the school, and driven away with him. Everybody was pretty sure they could still hear Elliot from several blocks away.

"Don't worry," Angie told Nelson when he showed back up. "Elliot asked the King for your head and other parts, but King D. told him absolutely not. The King said a good magician was just too hard to find."

"A good magician would still have three fish left," said Sidney, chuckling.

————

The Great Hall looked like a school cafeteria again now that everyone had left a mess.

"Those parents have no manners," Angie muttered, picking up dirty dishes.

"Yeah, but they sure have great kids," Philip said, and suddenly everyone was telling everyone else how terrific the evening had been, and how smart they were to think of it, and they all pretty well forgot that it had been Ms. D.'s idea to begin with.

There was a lot of moaning about it, but then they got busy scurrying around to clean up the cafeteria.

Queen D. took several of them down the hall to tidy the classroom too.

"I'm going to hate to take this off," she said a little wistfully, patting her crown as they walked. "I'm not sure when I'll get to be a Queen again."

Sidney walked beside her looking glum. Then he suddenly brightened up.

"I'll bring my crown back after Christmas vacation," he told her cheerfully. "Then I'll be the Only-King-Around."

"I hope the Christmas Spirit doesn't get lonely while we're gone," Angie told Adam Joshua while they worked. "I think I'll ask him to my house to eat on Christmas Day."

Adam Joshua was pretty sure the Christmas Spirit wasn't going to be too lonely.

He was just wondering if he should tell Angie that when King D. came in, slipped up behind the Queen, and pulled her into the coatroom.

They stayed in there a good long time.

"Come with me," Adam Joshua whispered to Nelson and Sidney, Heidi and Angie. He led them a few doors down the hall to the janitor's room. Inside, back in the corner, was another door.

"Stairs?" Angie said when they opened it. "Where do they go?"

Adam Joshua led them up the stairs, and they came out in an attic full of old school stuff.

"Hey," said Sidney, "I'll bet part of it's over the coatroom! And," he said slowly, thinking it through, "anybody who wanted to be a ghost could come up here to be one."

"I can't believe it," Angie groaned. "And I'll bet we know who wanted to be one."

They tiptoed across, and through a hole in the attic floor they could see a king kissing a queen.

"No fighting, no biting," Heidi giggled.

"Whoooooo's there?" Adam Joshua moaned in a creaky voice.

"Is now the time Sidney gets to take over as King?" Angie called down politely, and Sidney looked absolutely panicked.

It took the King a minute to stop kissing and answer them.

"Not a ghost of a chance," he said, chuckling in a very deep and familiar Christmas Spirit's voice.

He gave them a Royal Wink as he snapped off the coatroom light, and up in the attic a jester and a magician, a knight, a lady, and an Almost-King softly caroled down a terrific little Christmas song.

Don't miss:

The ADAM JOSHUA Capers

Nelson in Love

"Heidi's hair is the neatest color in the sun," Nelson said, "and it's always really shiny and everything."

Adam Joshua stopped in the middle of the sidewalk to stare at Nelson, but Nelson kept right on walking and talking about Heidi's hair until Adam Joshua had to hurry to catch up.

"And it smells just great, too," Nelson said with a sigh and a look in his eye that made Adam Joshua shiver clear down to his boots.